I'm going to read

UP TO
100
WORDS

I'm Going To READ!™

These levels are meant only as guides;
you and your child can best choose a book that's right.

Level 1: Kindergarten–Grade 1 . . . Ages 4–6
- word bank to highlight new words
- consistent placement of text to promote readability
- easy words and phrases
- simple sentences build to make simple stories
- art and design help new readers decode text

Level 2: Grade 1 . . . Ages 6–7
- word bank to highlight new words
- rhyming texts introduced
- more difficult words, but vocabulary is still limited
- longer sentences and longer stories
- designed for easy readability

Level 3: Grade 2 . . . Ages 7–8
- richer vocabulary of up to 200 different words
- varied sentence structure
- high-interest stories with longer plots
- designed to promote independent reading

Level 4: Grades 3 and up . . . Ages 8 and up
- richer vocabulary of more than 300 different words
- short chapters, multiple stories, or poems
- more complex plots for the newly independent reader
- emphasis on reading for meaning

Note to Parents

What a great sense of achievement it is when you can accomplish a goal! With the **I'm Going To Read!**™series, goals are established when you pick up a book. This series was developed to grow with the new reader. The vocabulary grows quantifiably from 50 different words at Level One, to 100 different words at Level Two, to 200 different words at Level Three, and to 300 different words at Level Four.

Ways to Use the Word Bank

- Read along with your child and help him or her sound out the words in the word bank.

- Have your child find the word in the word bank as you read it aloud.

- Ask your child to find the word in the word bank that matches a picture on the page.

- Review the words in the word bank and then ask your child to read the story to you.

Related Word Bank Activities

- Create mini-flash cards in your handwriting. This provides yet another opportunity for the reader to be able to identify words, regardless of what the typography looks like.
- Think of a sentence and then place the mini-flash cards on a table out of order. Ask your child to rearrange the mini-flash cards until the sentence makes sense.

- Make up riddles about words in the story and have your child find the appropriate mini-flash card. For example, "It's red and it bounces. What is it?"

- Choose one of the mini-flash cards and ask your child to find the same word in the text of the story.

- Create a second set of mini-flash cards and play a game of Concentration, trying to match the pairs of words.

LEVEL 2

2 4 6 8 10 9 7 5 3 1

Published by Sterling Publishing Co., Inc.
387 Park Avenue South, New York, NY 10016
Text © 2007 by Harriet Ziefert Inc.
Illustrations © 2007 by Rick Brown
Distributed in Canada by Sterling Publishing
c/o Canadian Manda Group, 165 Dufferin Street,
Toronto, Ontario, Canada M6K 3H6
Distributed in the United Kingdom by GMC Distribution Services,
Castle Place, 166 High Street, Lewes, East Sussex, England BN7 1XU
Distributed in Australia by Capricorn Link (Australia) Pty. Ltd.
P.O. Box 704, Windsor, NSW 2756, Australia

I'm Going To Read is a trademark of Sterling Publishing Co., Inc.

Library of Congress Cataloging-in-Publication Data

Hooray for the 4th of July! / pictures by Rick Brown.
    p. cm.—(I'm going to read)
  Summary: Illustrations and simple rhyming text describe the fun of a Fourth of
July parade.
  ISBN-13: 978-1-4027-4241-5
  ISBN-10: 1-4027-4241-X
  [1. Fourth of July—Fiction. 2. Parades—Fiction. 3. Stories in rhyme.]
I. Brown, Rick, 1946– ill.

PZ8.3.H773 2007
[E]—dc22   2006023417

Printed in China

Sterling ISBN-13: 978-1-4027-4241-5
ISBN-10: 1-4027-4241-X

For information about custom editions, special sales, premium and
corporate purchases, please contact Sterling Special Sales
Department at 800-805-5489 or specialsales@sterlingpub.com.

HOORAY FOR THE 4TH OF JULY!

Pictures by Rick Brown

Sterling Publishing Co., Inc.
New York

the   waiting   parade   in   begin

Everyone is crowding in,
Waiting for the parade to begin.

come   drum   will   and

Fife and drum, fife and drum,
Who will be the first to come?

favorite big here's reviewing stand

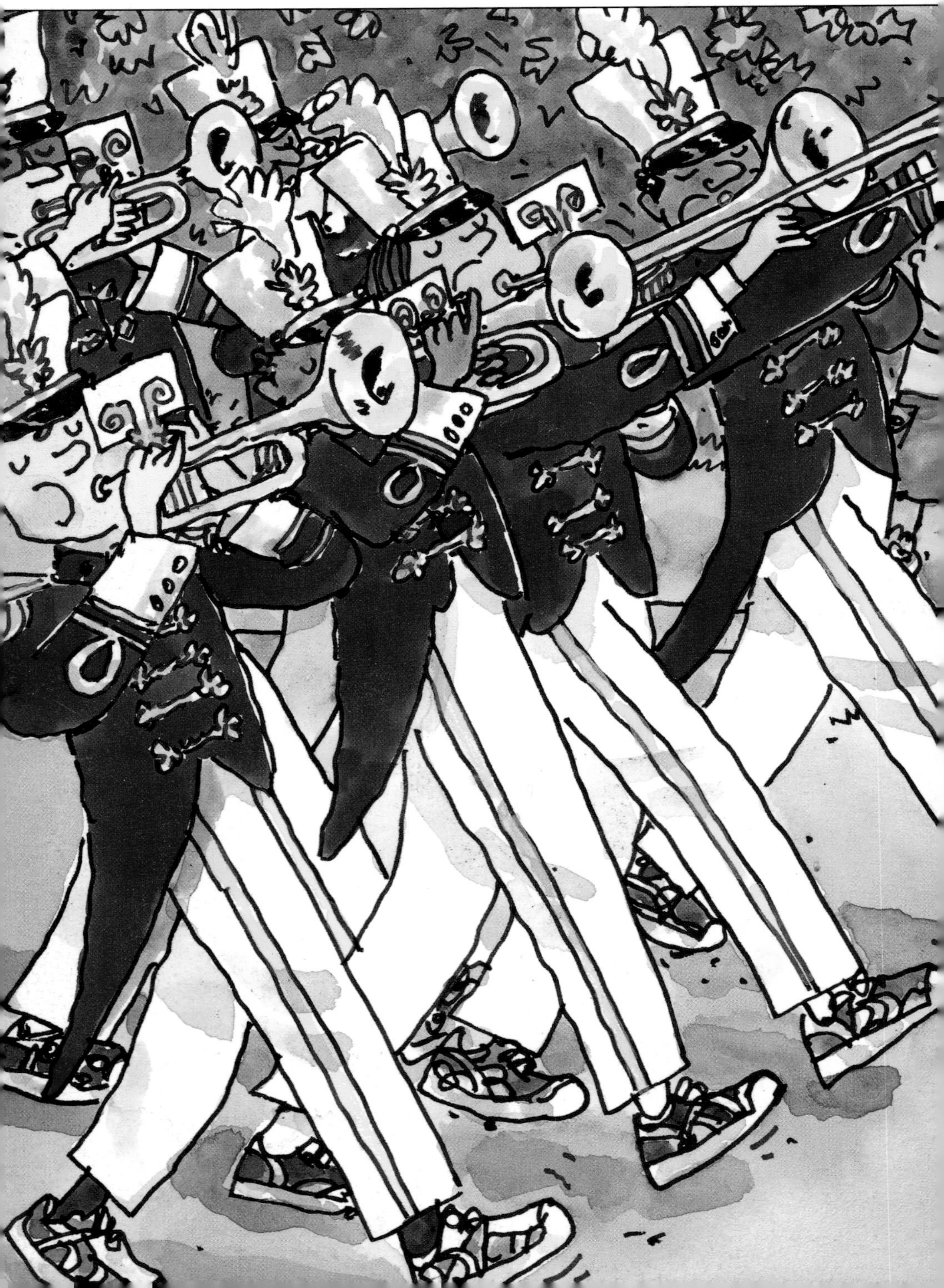

brass   our   passing   band   next

Here's our favorite big brass band,
Passing the reviewing stand.

Fife and drum, fife and drum,
Who will be the next to come?

The musicians' float rolls along.
Listen to their happy song.

Fife and drum, fife and drum,
Who will be the next to come?

High school kids on bikes ride by
With flags a-flying oh so high.

Fife and drum, fife and drum,
Who will be the next to come?

Next is the junior high school band.
Their uniforms look so grand.

Fife and drum, fife and drum,
Who will be the next to come?

Firefighters drive an old truck.
They wave a banner, "Lots of luck!"

Fife and drum, fife and drum,
Who will be the next to come?

Clowns on stilts throw confetti.
We wonder how they stay so steady.

Fife and drum, fife and drum,
Who will be the next to come?

Motorcycle police drive by last.

Now the whole parade has passed.

Boys and girls, a baseball team,

Everybody starts to scream.

Hooray!

Hooray
for the 4th of July!

Hooray!